The Twisted BRANCH

The Twisted BRANCH

By

Jeanne Storeim

Primix Publishing
East Brunswick Office Evolution
1 Tower Center Boulevard, Ste 1510
East Brunswick, NJ 08816
www.primixpublishing.com
Phone: 1-800-538-5788

Published by Primix Publishing: 05/23/2025

ISBN: 979-8-89194-468-8(sc)
ISBN: 979-8-89194-469-5(e)

Library of Congress Control Number: 2025909814

CONTENTS

CHAPTER 1

On the drive through the mountain landscape to her new home, Lauren reflects on leaving a successful career in accounting and city life for her new life as a fulltime artist and owner of a mountain retreat. She is looking forward to a peaceful and slower paced life in a rural setting. The lakeside lodge and cabins will provide her with income so she can fulfill her dream of spending her time creating stained glass art.

Snapping out of her daydreams, Lauren turns on her headlights as night is falling. The road seems to have gotten narrower with unexpected twists and turns. As she navigates out an especially sharp curve, she sees tail lights speeding off. She slams on her brakes before she runs over a large lump in the road. She pulls over and puts on her flashers before getting out of her car to see what is blocking the road. When she gets closer, she discovers, to her horror, that the lump is a dead man with a massive head wound.

She runs back to her car to call authorities only to find there is no cell service. In her rearview mirror she sees another vehicle approaching. The vehicle pulls up behind her and stops. She cautiously watches as a man climbs out of an old pickup. The man is tall and slender and is wearing bib overalls. He walks over and observes the body before coming back to where Lauren is standing next to her car. He introduces himself as Tom "the wood guy" in a quiet softspoken manner. He asks if she is ok and then tells her he has a CB radio and will contact the sheriff.

In a short time, police cars arrive with lights flashing. Two officers begin setting up lights and prepare to divert traffic around the body. Another officer approaches Lauren and Tom. He greets Tom by name and then turns to Lauren and introduces himself as Don Larson, the sheriff. He questions them and then tells them they are free to go but that he will be in touch with them in the next couple of days if he has any follow-up questions.

Lauren gets back in her car and continues on to the lodge.   When she pulls into the driveway, she is greeted by McKenzie, the lodge manager and her friendly golden retriever, Noah. They go into the great room of the lodge and seat themselves on the over-stuffed sofas in front of a crackling fire. Lauren then recounts the bizarre event causing the delay in her arrival. McKenzie expresses concern for Lauren and her surprise. She says , to her knowledge, nothing like this has ever happened here before. After a few more minutes of talking with McKenzie, Lauren goes to the comfort of her private quarters to get some sleep. She is exhausted after a full day of driving and the unexpected shock of finding a body on the road.

She finds herself restless and unable to drop off to sleep. She keeps thinking about the dead man. The part of her brain that processes logical thought keeps nagging at her that something is off and she keeps trying to understand what it is.

She finally drifts off into a sound sleep.

CHAPTER 2

Lauren wakes up to a bright sunshiny day. She showers and puts on jeans and a light sweater to keep off the morning chill. After looking in the mirror to check her make-up, she puts her long tawny hair in a ponytail and grabs a pair of sunglasses. She goes to the lodge and enjoys a steaming cup of coffee and a fresh oatmeal muffin in the dining room.

She decides to take a tour of her new home. She leaves the glass-walled dining room and steps out onto the large deck. The mountains, in brilliant fall colors, are reflected in the glassy surface of the lake. She goes down the steps from the deck and follows the path to the marina. There are three finger docks branching off the main dock which stretches straight into the water. The rental pontoons, kayaks and fishing boats are all tied to the finger docks awaiting customers. She continues along the path past the rustic cabins. The covered front porches have window boxes along the railings giving a cheery welcoming impression. They are all booked for the fall season and Lauren wonders what kind of guests will be staying in them.

She circles the cabins and heads back to the lodge. She loves the rustic look of the huge old log and stone lodge. Massive timbers make up the covered entrance. The expansive floor to ceiling windows of the lodge are framed by rock pillars which blend into the natural woods and rock outcrops surrounding the building.

She heads to her studio which is located at the far end of the lodge. She wants to see if any of her supplies have arrived and start unpacking. She enters her studio through the solid wood door and marvels at the brightly lit spacious room. Windows on two sides provide lots of light and the wood beams and floors soften it to a golden glow.

After spending some time organizing her studio, she walks to McKenzie's office for an update on the business of running the lodge. McKenzie is sitting behind her desk twirling a lock of curly red hair around her finger, concentrating on the paperwork in front of her. Noah, who is on his bed beside her desk, thumps his tail in welcome. When McKenzie sees Lauren, her face brightens up with a big smile and she gestures for Lauren to take a chair. They go through some details of the up-coming week. She is told a few of the guests will be here later in the day, but most of them will be arriving tomorrow. The weather forecast is perfect, and the guests have reserved boats and kayaks as well as spaces on buses and trams with local tour companies for fall foliage viewing. The brochure rack is fully stocked so those wanting to self-tour can easily find maps and information on local places of interest.

After having a quick lunch on the deck, Lauren decides to head to town. The town of Hawk's Mountain has a central square with the post office anchoring one corner. It is the focal point of the local community and is run by a third-generation member of the Harris family. Celia Harris is the congenial postmistress ands also source of information for everything that goes on in the area. Lauren steps in to check her P O box and meets Celia. Celia already knows all about the body found on the road. After Lauren introduces herself, Celia remarks on Lauren finding the body and continues with

"Some say it was murder you know."

When Lauren asks about Tom, Celia offers

"Everybody likes Tom. He's known as "the wood guy" around here. He can do anything with wood. He lives alone, you know. Been in that cabin behind your place for years."

Stepping out of the post office, Lauren glances around the square at the quaint small shops selling local handicrafts and the slightly larger stores selling necessities like hats and sunscreen. On the opposite side of the square is a prominent real estate office. The large front windows are lined with flyers for lavish mountain homes. Also featured is a picture of the broker. She has fashion model looks and clothes to match.

Lauren strolls around the square, stopping to browse at some of the shops. She selects some local honey and jams that she feels will be perfect for the ding room at the lodge. She also picks up some work gloves and shelf organizers at the hardware store for her studio. Just as she steps out of the hardware store, Madelyne, the real estate broker, stops her and introduces herself and continues with

"Hi, I am the gal who takes care of the people looking to make this beautiful place their home. Or second home. Or occasional retreat."

With a big smile she adds

"Do you have any friend from the city looking for the perfect escape?"

Then without waiting for an answer, she leans in for a quick perfectly executed air kiss and says

"Tata, must run. Let's do lunch and get acquainted soon."

Then she is gone, swiftly walking down the street.

Lauren feels almost like she has been hit by a tornado. A small tornado. But a tornado, none the less.

She is driving back home when it hits her! She knows what was nagging at her subconscious. Everyone she has seen, except for Madelyne whose business it is to relate to city people, is dressed for the outdoors. When she looked at the body he was dressed for city life. Loafers, linen slacks and a silk shirt.

Where did he come from and how did he end up here?

CHAPTER 3

After arriving back at the lodge Lauren delivers her goodies to the dining room. She decides another walk to get familiar with her surroundings would be a good way to end her first day. Going past the cabins she follows a dirt track into the trees. After a short distance she discovers a beautifully carved sign on a post. It says

TOM
THE WOOD GUY

As she ventures past the sign, she hears a loud noise. She sees Tom with a chain saw working on a wood sculpture. It is a partially finished soaring eagle and is unbelievably beautiful. Celia was right about his talent. Tom stops his chain saw when he sees Lauren. He greets her with a warm smile and invites her onto the porch of his log cabin for coffee. He serves her fresh ground coffee in unique pottery mugs. When she compliments him on the mugs, he tells her there lots of artists in the mountains. They often barter with each other and he got them from a friend and artist who is a potter.

When she tells him her story of moving to the lodge to devote herself to her art which is stained glass he offers to introduce her to his artist friends.

After thanking him for the coffee she departs for the lodge. She heads straight to her studio, excited to start working on new projects. She is imagining the first piece she wants to make with all the glowing fall colors. She thinks she may start with a lamp. She reminds herself to reach out to the gallery that shows her work to let them know she will have something available for them soon. After sorting through her glass inventory and choosing the colors she needs for her project Lauren locks her studio and heads for the main part of the of the lodge. When she arrives, McKenzie is at the front desk going over the guest list with the desk clerk. After finishing up at the front desk she, and the ever-present Noah, lead the way to her office to go over the list with Lauren.

The lodge has three suites booked.

Dr. and Mrs. Givens -A retired Dr and his wife are from Atlanta. They are looking for low-energy guided tours for leaf peeping.

Ms Adelle Lawrence – a retired fourth grade teacher and Ms Mary Pickerall – a retired third grade teacher are here to hike and visit some scenic overlooks and other places of interest designated by the park service. They have requested maps and brochures.

Don Overby - a retired window manufacturer- and his wife Glenda are amateur photograhers looking for colorful autumn and waterfall shots.

The cabins are all booked.

The two cabins farthest from the lodge are reserved for James and Crystal Sinclair and Mark and Susan Winters. They all have pressure-filled jobs and need a quiet place to unwind.

A fraternity and sorority reserved the remaining four cabins. They are all serious mountain hikers and are going to tackle some of the more advanced trails.

Everything is taken care of. Mr. and Mrs. Overby already checked in and everyone else is checking in tomorrow. McKenzie finishes with

"Looks like the last quiet night for a while. Enjoy it."

Early the next day Lauren goes to the police station in town. After a short wait, she gets in to see the sheriff. He was the officer who questioned her the night she found the body in the road. When she asks if they have identified the body, she is surprised to hear they do not have any word back yet on fingerprints or DNA tests. Also, no missing persons have been reported in the area and no matching description came up in the national database.

The sheriff wants to know if she can be more specific about the taillights of the fleeing vehicle or if she can remember anything else. He mentions there was a part of a log in the road in the vicinity of the body and asks if she remembers that. She says she remembers

Tom moving something off the road, but didn't see what it was.

The sheriff then tells her they are waiting on the autopsy report, but it looks like blunt force trauma to the head as the cause of death.

Lauren leaves the police station puzzled why they couldn't ID the body. She is also wondering why Tom moved something off the road that night.

She returns to the lodge to a flurry of activity with guests checking in. She hurries past the main part of the lodge for the quiet of her studio. She is glad to have a peaceful sanctuary to work in and starts cutting glass to fit the pattern for her new piece. The calm of the studio and familiarity of working in her element leaves her mind free to speculate on the identity of the body. Why can't they find out who he is? With all the technology available it seems odd to not have that part of the puzzle solved. She finishes cutting the glass pieces and lays them on the pattern she designed for the lamp. The golds, reds, and oranges will create an exceptionally warm light. She wants the lamp to have a wood base and thinks of Tom. She would love to talk to him about that and see what he thinks. She has seen his talent and knows he could create the perfect base for her.

Lauren goes back to the main lodge to check in with McKenzie. She finds her and Noah in the office.

McKenzie is busy on the phone. Lauren talks to Noah and gives his ears a scratch and his tummy a rub when he rolls onto his back. McKenzie hangs up the phone and says everything is a little hectic, especially with the surprise walk-in guest. She smiles when she notices Lauren petting Noah and remarks

"Looks like Noah has a new best friend."

She then asks if Lauren would do her a huge favor and take him out for a romp.

"He has been stuck inside with me most of the day and could use some outside time"

Lauren agrees and Noah jumps up excitedly when McKenzie hands her the leash. They head out and spend an hour exploring every moving leaf and mysterious tree hollow in the wooded area behind the lodge.   After one last sniff of the cool autumn air, it is time to take him back to his place beside McKenzie's desk.

On their way through the lobby, they see a muscular dark-haired man wandering around by the brochure rack. Noah, who is usually overly friendly, seems to sink down and lowers his ears. As the man approaches, Noah moves in front of Lauren as if to protect her.

The man introduces himself as Marty and tells her he has been wanting to come to this part of the country "forever". He adds how glad he is that they had a room for him. When she asks how he found the lodge he brushes it off with a vague reference to a travel site she has never heard of.

Just when she starts to walk away, he asks her if she is the one who found the body in the road. He goes on with

"What did she see? Did she know who it was? What did he look like?"

After telling him she only had a glimpse of the man and she really didn't know anything, he reluctantly lets her pass.

How odd. Why did he seem so interested?

CHAPTER 4

auren is surprised the next morning to have a message at the front desk from Madelyne.

"Can you meet me for lunch today at the quaintest little café in town? It's called Patti"s Cups and Cakes and is right on the Square by my office. See you noonish. Tata."

Lauren thinks this might be kind of interesting. Then she wonders what she should wear. Should she dress up or go with the local look and keep it casual. She decides she would come out looking like a poor second to Madelyne's sophisticated style if she dressed up so she decides on jeans a turtle neck and a black wool jacket.

She leaves around 11:30 for the short drive into town. After finding a parking spot near the square Lauren heads for the café to meet Madelyne. When she gets close, she spots her seated at a table by the window. When she walks in, she is greeted by the wonderful aroma of fresh baked goods.

Madelyne waves her over and greets her with an air kiss and then coos

"So glad you could make it. They have the yummiest baked goods here and the sandwiches are to die for." After being served coffee and ordering sandwiches. Madelyne politely asks her if she is settled in. She then says she would be glad to answer any questions about the area or the people.

"This is a pretty small place, so we all know each other. Except, that is, for the part time residents and the vacationers. Some of the part-time residents prefer their privacy and we respect their wishes on that. They support a lot of the trade people around here so we don't want to upset the apple cart."

As if to illustrate her point she goes on with

"I just got a call this morning to list an absolutely stunning home. I was a little surprised as the owners just bought the place this spring. Of course, I don't ask, but people from the city usually stick it out for at least two years if they find they really can't adapt to living in the country. The owners are really anxious to sell and are willing to take less than they paid .This is such a surprise. Especially considering how much they put into it after they bought it. They had Tom" The Wood Guy "build a woven wood railing for their deck. His work is fabulous and always one of a kind."

She looks at Laurena and asks

"Have you met him? He's quite a hunk, if you go for the mellow hippie type."

Without missing a beat, she then asks

"Do you want dessert? They have the best pie here."

Checking her watch, she grabs her purse and stands up saying

"Must run. So nice chatting. Don't worry, I've got the check. Tata."

Lauren watches her head out the door and again feels like she has been in the vicinity of a tornado. The impact is a little less than the first time so maybe she will eventually get used to Madelyne's high-energy encounters.

Lauren drives back to the lodge intending to spend the afternoon in her studio working on some new designs. Being surrounded by the natural beauty of the area has her head brimming with ideas for new projects. She is thinking of how she can make a series of suncatchers reflecting the seasons in the mountains. It might be a product that local shops would be interested in selling.

As she is walking to the back of the lodge and her studio, she sees Mr. and Mrs. Overby ahead of her in deep conversation. Not wanting to intrude, she slows down but can't help hearing Mrs. Overby strongly proclaim

"He would have been 24 this month. I miss him so

much and would do anything to get even with the person who did that to him.'

Mr. Overby responds calmly, acknowledging her feelings, but emphasizes the importance of continuing with their lives. Then they turn the corner to the lake. Lauren wonders what happened to this couple that could cause so much pain and anger. She resolves to do a google search to see if she can find out later.

After spending a very productive afternoon on the suncatcher series designs, she heads to the lodge to check in with McKenzie. Finding her in her office, she sits down and waits for her to complete what she is working on before getting the daily report on lodge business. As soon as she sits down, Noah comes and rests his head on her knee, looking up at her with his soulful brown eyes

McKenzie glances up from her paperwork and speaks

"He's working you, you know. He knows when he does that, he gets pretty much anything he wants. Right now, I think it is a treat."

They both laugh and Lauren reaches into the treat jar on the desk to fish one out. Noah immediately sits, with his tail wagging and a little bit of drool slipping out of one corner of his mouth. Lauren holds out the treat for him and he gently takes it from her hand and goes back to his bed beside the desk.

McKenzie sits back in her chair with a tired smile on her face.

Everything seems to be going well. All the guests are busy with tours and excursions during the day. Breakfast and dinner in the dining room have been very busy and may require some added part-time staff.

McKenzie looks at Lauren and muses

"There's a new act at the casino in Cherokee. Maybe we should take a break and go check it out. We could go and have an early dinner and catch the first act."

Lauren agrees and McKenzie gets online to check on ticket availability.

"Looks like we can get in tomorrow night. Should I book it?"

Lauren again agrees and after a brief conversation about what time to leave and what to wear she heads out to stroll around the property. As she passes through the great room the fraternity/sorority group of guests barrel through the main door. It sounds like they had a great day hiking to the tallest peak and they can't wait to compare cell phone photos over their campfire tonight. Right now, they are famished and charge towards the dining room.

Lauren reflects on her college days and thinks about

some of the friends she had back then. It might be fun to reach out to some of them. Maybe she could have an informal reunion at the lodge.

A walk along the dock as the sun is setting is glorious. She can't imagine living in a more beautiful place.

The boats and kayaks have all been secured for the night and the fishing guides are finishing up cleaning their boats and tackle and preparing for an early start tomorrow.

She decides to just grab some soup and biscuits from the dining room and take it to her living quarters for a quiet evening. As she is going through the dining room to pick up her food from the kitchen, she sees Mr. and Mrs. Overby at a table appearing to be In the middle of a serious discussion. As she passes their table she hears Mrs. Overby exclaim

"It's him! Can you believe he is here. I just wish he were dead!"

Her husband shushes her but Lauren can't unhear what was said. Wishing someone was dead seems like a pretty strong statement. What can they mean by "He's here?"

CHAPTER 5

The next day goes by quickly as Lauren coordinates her new suncatcher designs with the glass colors she has chosen. Pastels for spring, strong primary colors for summer, warm earthy tones for fall, and cool blues and whites for winter. As she checks her inventory, she realizes she needs to order more glass and solder and other miscellaneous supplies. Since they will be shipped to the post office, she reminds herself to let Celia know to expect them and see if she will call when they arrive.

By late afternoon, she is in her quarters getting ready for her outing with McKenzie. She is looking forward to seeing more of the regional landscape. She has picked out a long black form-fitting dress and adds a red silk kimono with gold cherry blossom embroidery. She adds some red chandelier earrings and black backless heels. She looks in the mirror and likes the bold colors combined with black. She hopes she isn't overdressed for the event.

As she is closing her door, she thinks about Mr. and Mrs. Overby and vows to do some google research tomorrow. Tonight is just for fun and new experiences.

She meets up with McKenzie in the lobby. McKenzie is wearing a long bottle green boho dress with a lace up bodice and a fairy hemline. Her long curly hair is pinned back on one side with a gold clip and cascades down her back. They compliment each other and get in McKenzie's car for the drive to the casino which is less than an hour away.

Pulling into the parking lot, they see the sheriff and a small group of men at the far end of the lot. When Lauren wonders out loud what could be going on, McKenzie, in her typical take-charge style, suggests they go find out. She has known Don, the sheriff, forever and feels comfortable asking him. As they approach, Don and the other men look up and their conversation comes to a complete stop. Clearly, the appearance of these two gorgeous ladies in elegant evening dress is quite a surprise. As soon as Don recognizes McKenzie a big smile appears on his face, and he steps forward to talk to her.

McKenzie, You look great! It's been a while since I've seen you.   So, what brings you here?"

McKenzie replies that they are taking the night off and are here for the show. She then adds

"I would introduce you to my new boss, but it seems you have already met." Don acknowledges this and greets Lauren with

"So nice to see you again."

He then turns to the man next to him. The man is well built and has a full head of eye-catching silver hair. The man doesn't have the same aura as the other policemen in the group but has a look of quiet authority about him. Don introduces him as Duncan, an associate and old friend. He adds

"He's here trying to clear up a mystery for us. We are tracking down the owner of a seemingly abandoned car and we need someone who can dig a little deeper than than our local resources.

Well ladies, have a fun evening and drive safely on your way home. "

With a sardonic smile at Lauren he adds

You never know what may pop up in the middle of the road."

As they proceed to the casino, Lauren is intrigued by the silver-haired man and his obvious access to information unavailable to regular law enforcement.

How intriguing.

The casino is an extreme change from the bucolic atmosphere that Lauren has become accustomed to since her arrival. The dining experience is first class and the show, although not nearly "Broadway" caliber, is well done.

On the way home Lauren asks McKenzie about Duncan. She can't seem to get him off her mind.

McKenzie tells her

"He has been around here for a few years. I am not sure what he does or did. I think he was in some kind government agency and is kind of retired. He has a home pretty far off the beaten path. I've never seen it, but heard it's pretty spectacular. We don't see him a lot, but he seems like a nice guy. Kind of mysterious, but really nice."

The rest of the ride back to the lodge was pretty quiet with both women content to reflect on the evening. Lauren is exhausted and glad to get home and settled in her bed. Just before she falls asleep she, once again, thinks how glad she ended up in this place.

The next morning, after a breakfast of fruit and a fresh muffin, Lauren heads to her studio. Today she is going to be spending time online catching up on correspondence and general business "housekeeping". After a couple of hours, she pauses to stretch. She remembers she wanted to do a google search on the Overby's and see if she can bring anything helpful to light. After a short search, she finds an article that explains the conversation she heard on the walkway.

They had a son who died tragically of a drug overdose. He had been a serious mountain biker and suffered a serious shoulder injury during an event. During his recovery he became addicted to pain killers. He was unable to overcome his addiction, and his death was a result of contaminated drugs he bought on the street. Lauren is saddened to learn the source of such despair but now understands their feelings.

She decides to take a break ands go into town to do a little more exploring in the local shops. She hopes she will find a place to sell some of her work. After browsing the shops along the square, she spots a place about a half block away that she hasn't been to. The outside has a variety of bright- colored metal art pieces and also some flags and wind spinners. Thinking this might be a good fit for her work she goes in to look around.

A disembodied voice greets her with

"Welcome to Savannah Hannah's"

She looks past a display of wind chimes and sees a woman with long blond hair filling a counter display. After thanking the woman for the greeting, she looks around the shop. It is filled with merchandise cleverly displayed to draw customer's eyes from the tiered shelving displays to an array of hanging wind chimes and mobiles.

When Hannah asks her if she is looking for anything in particular, Lauren explains she is pretty new to the area and just getting familiar with the town.

Hannah responds with

"Oh, you're the new owner of the lodge. I am Hannah and I am so glad to meet you. I hope you enjoy the shop. I carry a lot of work from the local art community here. "

Lauren is intrigued and asks how she chooses her handmade inventory, hoping to find a way to get her work in the shop.

Hannah answers with a friendly laugh

"Oh, that's easy. You buy me lunch and talk to me about your work."

Surprised by Hannah's easy-going approach to business, Lauren explains that she is a glass artist and is looking for a local outlet for her work,

Hannah reaches to the checkout counter and picks up a wildly colored business card. As she hands it to Lauren, she beams

"I thought I heard you were an artist. If you can send me some pictures of your work, that would be great. Oh, and of course, we will have to meet for lunch and work something out.:\"

As Lauren leaves, she marvels at her good luck in finding a possible location to sell her work.

She walks back towards the square and decides to

check with Don to see if he has any updates. She finds him sitting at his desk that is piled high with papers and folders. He looks up when she walks in and gestures her to a chair across the desk from him.

He starts with

"I think I may be making progress but, sometimes it feels more like one step forward and one step back. With a little help from our friends at the federal level we have identified the victim. It seems he is a known drug dealer by the name of Manny Ortiz. At least that was his name. His current name is Juan Mendoza, courtesy of the nice people who run the witness protection program. That's why it took so long for the identity to come through. Apparently, Manny was arrested on some serious charges and decided it would be in his best interest to give up some information as apposed to spending the next twenty or so years in a sunless environment.

Voila! Juan Mendoza

That was his car that we found at the casino.

So now, ALL we have to do is figure out why he was here and who killed him.

Manny worked out of Jersey but was relocated to Atlanta as Juan. How this all ends up here is the question. "

Smiling again he says

"So if you have any suspicious guests from Jersey or Atlanta I hope you will let me know. "

She informs him of the unexpected guest and tells him she will email his info from the check-in registry when she gets back to the lodge. She also tells him about Mr. and Mrs. Overby's conversations and what she found online.

He thanks her and tells her jokingly that she should be a detective.

As she is driving back to the lodge, she has a feeling in the back of her mind that this is all connected.

But How?

CHAPTER 6

Lauren spends the day in her studio working on her stained-glass lamp. As she works, she realizes she needs to talk to Tom and see if he will make a base for her lamp. Around four she decides to quit for the day and walk to Tom's. The weather is perfect, and she finds Tom outside working on a large wood bowl. He stops his wood tooling machine when he sees her. She admires the bowl, and he tells her it is from a 200-year-old tree that went down in a storm. He says he salvages most of the wood he uses.

"A lot of people know that I am always looking for wood, so they get in touch when they want trees removed."

When she tells him she would like him to create a base for her the lamp he invites her into his barn and tells her to look around. The rafters are brimming with all different sizes and shapes of long wood pieces. The walls are covered with spacious shelves full of shorter stockier chunks of wood.

He asks her about her project and what she envisions the end-product to look like. She tells him she pictures a mid-sized table lamp and would like the base to have a natural look to match the pattern in her shade.

He walks around and pulls two different pieces from the shelving. One is a round piece with a gold tone and several interesting looking knots. The other is darker and gradually twists from top to bottom. The twisting seems to have a flow Lauren thinks would be a perfect match for her leaf design.

She and Tom discuss the dimensions and move to a table where he has a large number of sketch pads and pencils. As he is working on a sketch for her, Lauren sees a sketch of what looks like a fence. Tom notices her interest and explains

"That is a work in progress. It is a natural wood deck railing."

She remembers Madelyne mentioning the house she listed with that type of railing.

Tom goes on to say he installed it at a home in the spring but somehow it became damaged and they need part of it replaced. He adds he can't imagine what could have happened. It was designed to withstand a lot of stress. They must have pushed something pretty heavy against it for it to give way.

She thinks this might be an improvement on the deck railing at the lodge. She tells him what she is thinking, and he says he will be working on the repair this week and invites her to the house to see the railing. He tells her the owners are out of town, so she won't be intruding on them. He adds, with a laugh that their crazy 120-pound rottweiler will also be absent which is a big relief to him.

She continues to look around the projects has laying around while he continues to work on the sketch. She is impressed by his range of skills. In a few minutes he says he isn't satisfied with the sketch he has and will keep working on it. If she wants to come to the house with the damaged railing, he will be there tomorrow. He will have a new sketch for her and she can examine the natural railing system as well. She agrees and he writes down the directions for her.

As she is walking home, she pictures a large angry rottweiler crashing through the railing. She wonders if that is even possible.

CHAPTER 7

The next morning, she checks with McKenzie to see if she needs to pick up anything for her and gives Noah a belly rub and a treat. She then checks at the front desk to be sure that the guest information has been sent to the sheriff.

She stops at the post office to check her mail and then heads to the sheriff's office. After checking in, she proceeds down the hall and taps lightly on Don's door. Just as she is about to go in, the door is opened by the silver haired man she met at the casino. She is impressed when he greets her by name and gestures her in with a smile. Keeping his hand on the door, he turns to Don and says,

"I'll do some research on my end and will let you know what comes up."

As he walks out, he says "Nice to see you again" to Lauren and is gone. Lauren is surprised at how pleased she is that he remembered her name.

She sits down and waits for Don to fill her in with any news, saying she hopes the info she sent was helpful. He replies that he hasn't had time to process it yet but will let her know. He tells her to keep him in the loop if anything else occurs to her.

Lauren leaves the building and gets in her car. After rereading the directions, she drives out of town to meet Tom and look at the deck railing design. She winds around some mountain roads and after several stops to check her directions she arrives at the house. She pulls into a short, curved driveway that divides into an upper and lower level. The lower-level winds down to an enclosed garage and the upper level leads to the main entrance of the house.

It is a beautiful log home in a light honey color and has a large double door entryway. As she approaches the doors, she sees a note stuck to one of the panels. It instructs her to follow the path around the house and come out to the deck. She follows the flagstone path to the back of the house. As she steps up on the deck she is amazed, not only by the size of the house, but also that it has been carved into the hillside. The entrance is at ground level and the back of the house is overhanging a large deep valley. The view is spectacular.

Tom is at the edge of the deck surrounded by an assortment of tools and what looks like tree branches. She walks over to the edge of the deck skirting the obstacle course of curving twisted branches. When she looks down, she sees the edge of the concrete pad from the garage below and a curving ditch filled with large boulders going down the steep slope.

Tom comes to stand beside her and thanks her for taking the trouble to come. After listening to her marvel at the house and the views Tom brings out the sketch he made for her lamp. It is better than she imagined. It has a divided base that looks like the ending of the root system evolving into a trunk that twists upward into what would be the leaf canopy which will be her shade.   After discussing some different stain options, they go to take a close look at the natural deck railing.

Lauren is intrigued that the branches so seamlessly entwine. Tom details how he first constructs the framework, according to code, for stability. He then begins the process of fitting the seemingly random branches into a woven network.

They examine deck, panel by panel, until they reach the missing portion. Lauren experiences a slight feeling of vertigo when she sees the open space with the drop down into the valley below. Directly below the damaged area is the rocky ditch. When she asks Tom about it, he tells her it is to funnel the runoff from the rain to avoid erosion. She can see where this would be good, given the cloudbursts the area gets in the summer,

Just when they are about to turn away, Lauren takes one more look at the opening and the rocky area below. She stops when she sees something sparkling between some of the rocks. When she points it out, Tom sees it too. He says when he first came to redo the broken rail he went down there to see if he could salvage some of the branches but didn't see it from the ground. He suggests that she stay on the deck and he will go down to retrieve whatever it is. He will need her to guide him to it since it would be hard to spot at ground level.

When he arrives at the ditch Lauren directs him to the place where she sees the reflection. Tom finds a gold chain wedged between some rocks. He reaches down between the rocks and when he brings his hand out, he is holding a medallion attached to the chain. Tom is curious by the find and starts a more thorough search of the area. He doesn't find any more jewelry but does find that it looks like some of the rocks have been moved and sees some brown stains on some of the others.

He makes his way up to the deck where Lauren is impatiently waiting. They examine the medallion and find it has a religious motif on one side and engraving on the other side. The engraving is faint with wear. There are some small letters they can't make out but the larger letters are perfectly legible, Theyn clearly spell out Manny!

CHAPTER 8

Lauren is stunned and explains to Tom the name is the same as the dead man they found on the road. After a short discussion they decide they need to call Don. Lauren gets through to Don on her cell phone and he says he will come up and take a look. While they are waiting they hash over the night they found the body on then road. During the course of their discussion, Lauren mentions that she thought she saw Tom move something off the road. Tom says that when he went to look at the body, he also took a look at the log in the road. It was a tree that had fallen due to disease. He explained that it is pretty common. They develop a disease that makes them rot from the inside out. When you look at the tree you may not realize that it is hollow on the inside due to the disease. All that is supporting the tree is a thin layer on the outside trunk. He says that when he looked at the tree on the road, all that was left was some pieces from the outside of the trunk. He also said that on his way back to his truck he saw a tarp partway in the ditch. He picked it up and stuffed it under some heavy pieces of wood in the back of his truck so it wouldn't blow out. He ends with

"Guess it's the environmentalist in me, I just couldn't leave a large piece of litter laying there."

When Don gets there, they give him the medallion which he places in an evidence bag before putting it in his pocket. He goes down to the ditch with Tom to take a look at the area where they found the medallion and the stains.

Lauren watches from the deck as they slowly examine the area below. After examining the rocky area, they walk slowly along each side of the ditch. They find an area with some footprints and a spot that looks like the soil has been disturbed.

When they get back up to the deck Don tells Lauren the stains look like dried blood and the grassy area has what looks like drag marks.

Don calls dispatch and requests crime scene techs to come out to the house and process the scene.

"They can paint a pretty good picture of what happened here." He says and then excuses himself to make some calls to locate the homeowners and get some background information on them.

Tom says he is going to stick around to see if he can help while Lauren decides it would probably be better if she left so she won't be in the way.

On her way home Lauren decides to do another google search. This time she wants to find out more about the victim.

CHAPTER 9

When she gets to the lodge Lauren checks un with McKenzie. It seems the two retired schoolteachers, Adell Lawrence and Mary Pickerall, stopped in the office earlier with some pictures they want McKenzie to look at. They are excited as they think they have found a patch of ginseng. McKenzie, being a local, knows all about wild ginseng and confirms their find. She asks the if they marked or disturbed their find and is relieved to hear they have read up on the "black gold" in this part of the mountains and left it undisturbed. They inform her they would not divulge its location as they know how endangered it is. They are just excited to have found it. Lauren is happy to hear the guests are having such a good time.

She is hungry so she orders a sandwich from the dining room and picks it up on her way to her studio. When she gets there, she grabs a drink out of the half fridge and settles into the chair at her computer desk. She unwraps her sandwich and opens her drink before opening her browser and starting her search on Manny Ortiz/New Jersey. After narrowing down the possibilities, she starts sorting through the info. She realizes she needs to narrow her search further, so she searches for drug arrests with that name. She is rewarded with an article about the arrest of Manual Ortiz on drug charges and even better, a picture. She can't believe her eyes; the picture looks exactly like the mysterious last minute guest Marty!

She decides to keep digging and see what she can find. Ortiz is a pretty common name, and she is overwhelmed by the amount of information. She then tries Manny and Marty on Facebook, but no luck there.

Next, she decides to try her luck with the homeowners from the crime scene house. She knows from her conversation with Madelyne their names are Johnny and Angela Rossi. She comes up with a lot of small pieces on them. It seems Johnny had a small plumbing business in Trenton and Angela had a hairdressing salon. Judging by the information she finds on social media it appears they were just a working-class couple. Then toward the end of 2021 their social media posts dry up. She can't find anything after that time frame.

How could they suddenly pop up here and buy a million-dollar property?

She decides she is going to leave this to Don, as he has much broader resources.

She enjoys a leisurely meal and a quiet evening reading in her quarters before going to bed early.

CHAPTER 10

In the morning the logical accountant side of her brain is once again nagging at her. It is giving her a strong urge to find the common link in all this. When she thinks about it, she realizes the common denominator for most human behavior is money. Definitely not a new idea, but maybe instead of trying to make a bunch of pieces of a puzzle fit she needs to look at it from a different perspective. As the say" Follow the money."

Back in her studio, she tries a different type of search. Using the skills she acquired from years of digging up information for clients to complete their financial reports, she starts looking at Manny and Marty and Rossi's. Here she is in her element.

It appears Manny had a pretty nice lifestyle with no discernable means of income. Not surprising, as he was in the illegal drug business. Nice cars, frequent travel and a second house on the Jersey shore until the arrest date-then nothing. Enter Juan Mendoza, AKA Manny . Steady low paying job, low living expenses. No red flags there.

When it comes to Marty Ortiz she finds he is Manny's younger brother. His picture is almost identical to Manny's. Not much to find on him. He seems to have lived in his older brother's shadow. Same addresses, same lack of verifiable income.

One difference- no arrest record.

When she dives into her research on Johnny and Angela Rossi things get interesting. They are in their mid-thirties and their financial history is predictable as clockwork until the same time as their withdrawal from social media. They spent their lives making a modest income from their businesses. Then about late 2021 there is a huge influx of cash.

As an accountant, Lauren recognizes they have found the holy grail of grifters and desperate middle class businessowners. PPP Loans. The government was so proud to be helping small businesses they completely abolished any fact checking on applications. That is why millionaire sports stars and small failing businesses alike could get laughably large forgivable loans if they could muster up some creative writing skills. Looks like Johnny and Angela both passed this test with flying colors.

No wonder they decided it would be more fun to live in a mansion in the mountains instead of slogging to work in Jersey every day.

CHAPTER 11

She decides to give Don a call and tell him what she has found. When she gets him on the line, he sounds a bit harried. She tells him she has done some research and has some interesting information to share. He excuses himself saying

"Hold on a sec."

When he gets back on the phone, he tells her he is tracking something down and can't meet her but wants Duncan to come to the lodge and go over it with her. She is surprised but agrees to meet with him. She quickly goes to her quarters and pulls on some clean jeans and a crisp white shirt and black vest. She adds a little more mascara and pulls her hair out of the ponytail. She runs a brush through her hair and checks herself in the mirror before heading to the great room in the lodge. When she checks at the desk, she finds Marty has requested late maid service for his room, so he is presumably sleeping in.

Just as she is finishing up at the front desk, Duncan walks through the door. She goes to meet him and can't help but notice, aside from being awfully good looking, how he gives off the vibes of quiet confidence. After greeting him, she leads him outside around the lodge to her studio.

He tells her he is impressed with the lodge and hopes she is planning to stick it out for the long run. He adds

"Lots of people come here and find rural living too much of an adjustment. "

She tells him she is totally committed to her new lifestyle and has no intention of returning to the city. She asks him where he was from before moving here. He tells her he came from the DC area but traveled quite a bit.

After they enter her studio, Duncan looks around and expresses interest in her work. She says she is just getting settled and doesn't have anything completed yet. He replies he would like to come back when she has some finished pieces as he is looking to add some color to his home and thinks some glass art would be a good fit. She is pleased that he is interested in her work and is even happier that he will be coming back.

She leads him to her computer station and after pulling out a chair for him she opens the files where she has saved the information. He is impressed with her work and tells her she would be a great asset to a whole variety of government agencies. He says with a smile

"You know, the ones that are referred to by just their initials."

He doesn't seem surprised by much on Manny and Marty. He is glad to hear that Marty is still at the lodge and mentions he may want to talk to him before he leaves.

When they move on to the Rossi's information , he gets very interested. He asks her where the idea to do a financial search came from. She laughs and says that she had been an accountant for years and that part of her brain won't turn off. They go over the information she has, and he asks her some questions about how she would go about tracking the Rossi's spending after they moved here. She tells him she would have to get access to their bank and credit card accounts. She could then start building a pretty good picture of their habits and predicted spending from that. He asks her if she will do that if he gets her the information. His eyes light up when she tells him she can start as soon as she gets the information she needs.

They push their chairs away from the desk and he asks her if she can check with the front desk to see if Marty is still in his room. When Lauren calls, the desk clerk informs her tha Marty is in the dining room having breakfast. Duncan excuses himself to go to the ding room to talk to Marty but says he will get back to her soon.

CHAPTER 12

arty is sitting at a small table overlooking the lake with a steaming cup of coffee in front of him. When Duncan walks in he takes one look and the color drains from his face. He is all too familiar with the look of the man approaching him. He has been on the streets his whole life and knows the look of authority when he sees it. He heaves a sigh and resigns himself to the fact that he is about to have a conversation he isn't going to like.

Duncan pulls up the chair across the table and introduces himself. He goes on to say that he is helping the sheriff with an investigation and needs to clear a few things up with Marty. He suggests they go out on the deck, so they won't disturb the other guests. They walk out on the deck and both men lean on the railing overlooking the water.

Duncan asks Marty if he knows why he wants to talk to him and Marty shakes his head and replies

"Not really."

Duncan then asks if Marty has been in touch with his brother. Marty says his brother disappeared years ago.

Duncan then straightens and turns to Marty with a serious expression and starts talking. He explains he knows all about Manny/AKA Juan. He tells Marty he also knows it is no coincidence that he is here. He says he has some information about Manny and needs Marty to clear up some details before he is willing to share.

Marty hangs his head and dully says

"It was Manny, wasn't it? The body on the road. "

When Duncan nods, Marty seems to shrink in on himself and murmurs

"I thought so. I was hoping it wasn't, but deep down I guess I knew. "

Duncan gives him a minute and then replies

"Ok, Marty, you need to tell me what is going on. We need to find out what happened to Manny and right now you are the best lead we have. "

Then Marty starts talking

"Manny called about a week ago and said he found some "golden geese" and he was going to crack himself a couple of eggs. That's what he used to say if we found someone we could lean on and make a few bucks. He wanted to meet me here, so I told him I'd come. Just like always. He always had the ideas, and I always went along. Anyway, he said he would call in a couple of days and we would get together and he would tell me his plan. We always kept in touch. We used burner phones so no one could track us.

When I got here, I heard about them finding a body on the road.   I tried to find out what I could without anybody getting suspicious.

I kept waiting for Manny to call but he never did. If he were OK he would have called. He always took care of me. I didn't really have a plan, I was just waiting to hear from Manny. "

He continues with

"Then I get a call from Shirley. She's kind of my girlfriend. She wants to know when I will be home. She says I wasn't supposed to be gone this long, and I better get home pretty soon or she is going to throw my stuff out on the street. She says the rent is due and I know she can't afford it so I better get back. She just works for the veterinarian, and he doesn't pay her hardly anything.   Even when he calls her in the middle of the night for an emergency. Some people have a rottweiler that is like their baby, and it is in pretty bad shape. It needed emergency surgery to repair a broken shoulder and some other stuff. They didn't say why they waited a whole day to bring it in. It seems they knew the vet and knew he could fix their "baby". They even paid cash, which was kind of weird considering how expensive it was. She says it would be nice if we had that kind of money. "

Marty went on with

"So here I am waiting for a brother who isn't going to call and a girlfriend who is throwing me out on the street."

Duncan puts his hand on Marty's shoulder to give him some measure of comfort. He then tells him they need to go to the sheriff with this information. He reassures him he is no in trouble, but that he needs to talk to the sheriff.

Marty agrees and they move towards the door. On the way out Duncan stops by the desk and gives the clerk on duty his card and asks her to have Lauren Call him later.

CHAPTER 13

When they get to the sheriff's office Don is waiting for them as Duncan had called ahead to let him know they were coming. Don has Marty go over his story again then he asks Marty if he or Manny knew anyone in the area. Marty says he doesn't and has no idea why Manny wanted to meet here. Then Don shows Marty the medallion and Marty identifies it as his brother's. He reaches under his shirt collar and pulls out a medallion that matches the one in Don's hand. Marty says his mother gave them to the boys and they both always wore them. Marty goes on to say they are St Christipher's medals. His mother was a devout Catholic and believed this would help protect them when they left home.

Don asks Marty if he knows John and Angela Rossi. Marty says he has heard of them but doesn't know them. He remembers them because they grew up in the same neighborhood, but they were a little older than he was. He then says there were rumors that they came into a lot of money and left town.

Don asks if he thinks Manny knew them since Manny was more their age. After thinking it over for a minute Marty says he probably did. After a few more questions, they tell Marty can go but that he needs to stick around for a few more days until they can get this cleared up.

After Marty leaves Don and Duncan go over what

they have learned and start to put the pieces together. Don says his people think the Rossi's property was probably where Manny died. The blood on the rocks in the drainage ditch is his and so is the medallion. They can't explain everything, but think Manny was pushed against the railing with enough force for it to give way. He fell and was killed when he landed on the rocks. It looks like his body was then dragged up to the parking area by the garage. That's where the evidence would end, except for the fact that Tom showed Don the tarp he picked up beside the road the night they found the body. He had forgotten about it until he and Lauren were talking about that night. It was still stuffed under some things in the back of his truck. After testing it, they found Manny's blood on it. When they tested for prints Johnny and Angela's prints were all over it.

Don continues with

"We can probably assume they put a tarp in a vehicle to prevent any blood from getting on the interior and loaded the body into it. "

The rental they found in the casino parking lot was in Manny's name. Don had the techs go over it again. This time they concentrated on the cargo are area and found traces of the tarp lodged in the latch in the back hatch. His techs told him it looked like part of the tarp was in the latch when it was closed. When asked, they said it was very likely that the latch didn't lock, and the rear door could have popped open if it was jarred. Like by running over a bump. Given how slippery the tarp was, with any sudden braking and acceleration the tarp would have slid out of the vehicle. When Don finished sharing his information, Duncan brings him up to speed on what Lauren has found.

When you add all of this up in addition to what Marty told them it looks like the Rossi's were involved in Manny's death and tried to get rid of the evidence.

Don asks one of his staff to check with the veterinarian in Jersey and see who brought in the injured dog. He suspects the Rossi's put their injured pet in their vehicle and Manny's body in the rental. They must have been trying to get away from their house and dispose of Manny's body. When they hit the fallen tree the latch on the rental popped open. They couldn't stop as there was a car approaching from behind them. They dump the rental at the casino thinking it won't be noticed for a while and keep going. Their dog needs a vet but they can't go anywhere local. They know what the local gossip grapevine is like and can't take that risk.

They head for familiar territory to figure out what to do next.

CHAPTER 14

The next day Lauren's phone rings and it is Duncan. He asks if she can come to the station and talk to Don. She agrees and says she will head that way now.

Don is wondering why Duncan would want Lauren to come in. Duncan says he found it interesting when she explained how she could use past financial information to create predictable spending behavior patterns. Since they have no idea where the Rossi's are, this might be a way to get a lead on them.

Don is surprised and says

"I told her she should be on the force."

Duncan laughs and responds with

"Funny, I told her the Feds would love to have her on their team."

Don immediately puts in a call to access the Rossi's financials. He hopes the fact that they are people of interest in a suspicious death will expedite the process.

When Lauren arrives, they fill her in on what they have put together so far. They tell her they have a search in place for the Rossi's but wonder if she will take a look at the financial info when it gets in and share any insights she may have. Lauren tells them she will be glad to help and after a few more minutes of general conversation she leaves. She goes back to the lodge and walks towards McKenzie's office. She sees the Overby's at the desk and they seem quite distraught. As she gets closer to the desk, she hears the Overby's telling the clerk that they won't stay in the same place as the man who murdered their son. She realizes they are referring to Marty.

She quickly approaches the Overby's and tells them she has information they need to hear. They head over to the seating area by the large fireplace. When they are settled, she starts by telling them she knows about their son. She then goes on to tell them she made the same mistake about Marty when she was researching his brother Manny. They are shocked by this. Lauren then fills them in on the fact that she was the one who found the body on the road, and it turned out to be Manny. She says she somehow got more involved in the case and was trying to learn more about the victim. During her online research she came across a picture of Manny and she also thought it was her lodge guest. It was only after more digging that she realized her mistake.

Mr. Overby gently pats his wife's shoulder as she softly sobs. She utters

" I feel awful about the things I said. He was a bad man, but I never should have said the things I did."

Lauren tries to console her by saying her words didn't

have anything to do with what happened. She tells them she understands if they want to cut their vacation short and will accommodate them any way she can.

After the conversation with the Overbys, Lauren leaves for her studio. She is glad to have her work to distract her from all the events that are unfolding around her. She spends the rest of the day working on more designs for her series of suncatchers. The work clears her mind, and she feels refreshed as she finishes up her day.

She closes her studio and thinks she will take a walk along the lakeshore to enjoy the sunset. On the way she stops in the office to check in with McKenzie and see if Noah wants to go for a romp. McKenzie informs her the Overby's have decided to stay and even apologized to the desk clerk for their behavior. Lauren grabs Noah's leash and hooks him up for their walk. They enjoy a beautiful fall sunset and after an hour they return to the lodge. She drops Noah off and after stopping in her quarters for a book she goes to the dining room for a leisurely dinner. The crowd has thinned out and she sits at a small table enjoying the twilight. She has a great meal of roast beef with potatoes and baby carrots with a slice of apple pie for dessert. Later when she is in her room she wonders if she will hear from Don tomorrow and, if so, will Duncan be around.

CHAPTER 15

The next morning is bright and sunny so Lauren takes her coffee out on to the deck to enjoy. The property is bustling with people lining up on the docks to go out for a day of fishing or kayaking. The kitchen is delivering the box lunches to the different groups and it reminds Lauren to check what goes into the lunches to see if they need improvement. As she is thinking about this her phone rings. She sees it is Don and quickly answers. He has gotten access to the Rossi's financials and asks if she will take a look at them today. When she tells him she is looking forward it he says he will get someone to bring them out to the lodge for her. He thanks her and hangs up. She stops at the desk and instructs them to send the messenger from the sheriff's office to her studio. When she gets to the studio, she leaves the door open so the messenger can come in when they arrive. She has just finished getting her computer running and the list of programs she will be using opened when she hears a soft knock on the door. When she turns, she is pleasantly surprised to see Duncan standing there. He grins and says today his function is to be the messenger. They both laugh and he walks over and pulls up a chair next to hers and hands her a folder. She opens it and scans the documents. She is happy to see that she has a lot of information to work with.

She tells Duncan it is going to take a while, so she doesn't know if he wants to wait. He responds that he is going to stick around. He doesn't want to hover though, so he will go have breakfast and take a walk around the property. As soon as he leaves, she lays out the information and starts inputting the data. It is a tedious process, but she starts to see spending patterns developing. She sorts the information into a variety of different accounting systems so she can see the usual expense patterns and spot any anomalies.

After spending a couple of hours assigning expenses to different categories, she sorts the items that are common for everyday life and other items that draw a picture of each person's lifestyle. It is surprising how much you can learn about a person when you analyze their spending habits.

It looks like Johnny spends money on a monthly membership to a sports analytics site. The reasonable conclusion is that he has more than a passing interest in the outcome of sporting events. In short, this would indicate he is either using a bookie or spending time somewhere to access sports betting.

Angela has a history of extensive spa and beauty treatment establishments. Lauren thinks that their move to the mountains left her with very few options for those kinds of services.

 Given the number of establishments that could serve both of their needs, she comes up with the idea that there is only one place in the area that would satisfy both of them.

The casino.

Inspired by this thought she looks more carefully at ATM withdrawal locations. She sees a pattern of large and frequent withdrawals at the casino in Cherokee.

She spends more time tying up more loose ends but thinks the casino lead is something Don can use.

She leaves her office to look for Duncan. She finds him by the lake playing fetch with Noah. She is glad to see he is a "dog" person. She has never been able to understand people who don't like dogs.

When he sees her, he throws the stick for Noah and turns to meet her. When she tells him she has some information that might be useful he suggests they take it to Don at his office.

Duncan takes Noah back to McKenzie while Lauren goes to her studio to pick up the information she has printed out.

She meets Duncan in the parking lot to ride into town with him. He is waiting beside a very nice 4-wheel drive truck. When she admires his choice of vehicle he responds with

"Thanks"

and then adds

"When you live up here, you never know when you may need to go off the road."

They get to Don's office and gather around his desk to go over the reports Lauren has created. It looks like the Rossi's have developed a pretty lavish lifestyle. They concentrate on the casino angle and Don is excited to have something he can sink his teeth into. He surmises that since they are not here in the mountains and have left their dog at the vets in Jersey it would be logical to look for them there.

He thanks Lauren profusely for her help and tells them he is going to get to work on this and will be in touch as soon as he has something.

CHAPTER 16

Lauren tries to concentrate on work but finds herself too restless. She decides to take a walk down the lane to see Tom. She wants to see if he has had time to work on the lamp base. As she approaches, she sees him moving around inside the barn. When she gets to the door, he notices her and waves her in. He tells her he has the base for her and if it meets with her approval all he has to do is apply the stain.

She can't believe how beautiful it turned out. The lines in the wood seem to flow inward from the root-like base and then expand out to create the illusion of branches. He has somehow accentuated all the wood tones in the grain. The contrast in tones gives the wood a three-dimensional look she had not imagined. They pick out a stain color and decide a semi-gloss finish will give it the most depth. They then have a short discussion on the hardware for the lampshade. Tom promises to bring it to her studio in the next day or two when the finish has had a chance to completely dry.

Lauren walks slowly back to her studio to put the finishing touches on her lampshade. She is excited about being this close to completing her first project in her new surroundings. The rest of the day flies by. She plans how to set up the lighting for photographing her new piece. She knows the photography must be done well to present her work to the gallery. She reflects on how the image of your work is just as important when dealing with a gallery as the work itself. You can have an outstanding piece but if your presentation to the gallery is not top notch, they may not accept it.

This gets her to thinking about marketing to galleries nearer to her new home. She smiles as she realizes this means a road trip!

CHAPTER 17

The next day Lauren starts working on some sketches of other large pieces for the gallery. At noon she takes a well- deserved break. As she is eating her lunch on the deck her phone rings. It is Don. He sounds excited and tells her if she can come into his office he has some great news.   Lauren hurriedly finishes her lunch and goes to her quarters to change out of her work clothes. She puts on a light blue shirt and clean jeans topped with a soft leather jacket. She then gets into her car and heads into town. On the way, she wonders what Don has found out. She hopes the information she gave him helped.

She enters Don's office to find Don and Duncan leaning back in their chairs. They both look like the cat that swallowed the canary. After pointing Lauren to the remaining chair, Don leans forward with a gleam in his eye and says

"You really ought to consider a career in law enforcement. Thanks to you, we have busted this thing wide open."

He tells her that using the information she gave them they tracked the Rossi's to a casino in Atlantic City. They were preferred customers there so when they checked in they were comped a room. That's why when we sent out a search at all the hotels they didn't show up.

Our friends from Jersey sent a couple of guys to pick

them up. By the time they got them to the station they were more than ready to talk.

It seems Manny ran into them at the casino at Cherokee. The Rossi's were surprised to see him and knew about his past but put it all that aside. They were just glad to see someone from the old neighborhood to talk to. They spent some time together at the casino and before parting ways exchanged phone numbers. A few days later Johnny decides to give Manny a call and invite him to the house for drinks. That gave Manny a chance to check with some friends back home and find out how the Rossi's were living so large. When he realized how much money they had gotten from their PPP scam it was just natural for him to try to figure out how to get a piece of it. He planned to shake down the Rossi's to the tune of a million bucks. After all, look at how much they got. The Jersey police got this information from an informant that they worked with on a regular basis. Manny bragged to his buddies in Jersey that he would threaten to turn the Rossi's in if they balked.

When he arrived at their place he was impressed with the huge home. After being invited in they wandered back and forth between the deck and the kitchen to get more drinks. Manny was at the kitchen island getting a refill when he laid out his extortion demands. Johnny, who had always had a short fuse, exploded and started screaming. Angela tried to calm him down but he stomped out of the room returning a moment with a handgun saying he was going to blow Manny away. Manny turned and ran out the door to the deck. When he started running Rosie, the rottweiler, went into full attack mode and charged Manny. Just when they reached the edge of the deck Rosie launched all 120 pounds of canine fury at Manny. The force sent both Manny and Rosie through the railing.

By the time the Rossi's got to the edge of the deck and looked down Manny was lying completely still on the rocks and Rosie was on the berm just past the the ditch whimpering. The Rossi's both raced down to the ditch and found Manny had his head smashed by the rocks and was dead. Rosie was alive but was unable to get up or walk. They panicked when they realized how bad the situation was. They knew that if they called the police an investigation would follow and they would be exposed and would face criminal charges for fraud. They had to figure out how to get the body away from the property and get Rosie the help she needed.

They thought if they took Manny's body to the casino and left it in his car in the parking lot no one would notice it for days. They didn't care what the police thought as long as they were not connected. They would go right from the casino to a veterinarian they knew in Jersey. They knew they could lay low in a casino up there until Rosie was better.

They got a tarp from the garage and hauled Manny's body up to his car. The cargo area in the car was small and they had a hard time getting the tarp wrapped body to fit. Then they loaded Rosie into the back of their SUV. They cleaned up the evidence of their drinking party and grabbed a few clothes and took off. Johnny was in the lead in the SUV and Angela was driving Manny's car with the body.

They were driving through a heavily wooded stretch of road on their way to the casino when Johnny saw a fallen log. He swerved and missed it but Angela hit it head-on. It caused the car to land heavily after going over the fallen tree and the impact popped the back hatch open. Angela saw headlights in her rearview mirror and knew she had to get away. She sped up and after a few tense minutes she didn't see any more lights in the rearview mirror. She flashed her lights signaling Johnny. He found a side road and turned in and Angela followed. When they discovered the body had fallen out of the car, they knew they had to drop the car at the casino pronto and get leave the area fast.

They dropped the car as planned and then drove straight though to Jersey. On the way they decided to sell their house in the mountains. They wanted nothing more to do with the mountains or their house. At that point they thought they would stay in Jersey until Rosie could travel and then find someplace to start over.

CHAPTER 18

on ended the story with a big smile and said he didn't think Rosie would be charged. He added the Rossi's were under investigation for PPP fraud and things didn't look good for them, but it was better than being charged with murder.

He thanked both Lauren and Duncan for their help and looked at the piles of paperwork on his desk with a sigh. He said it would probably take days to get it all sorted out and he better get started on it.

Duncan and Lauren walked out to the sidewalk. Lauren was glad she helped get the mystery solved, but she regretted that she wouldn't be seeing Duncan anymore.

Just as she was about to tell him good-bye, he turned to her with a grin and said

"Ever been off-roading?"

And they both headed for his truck.